# The Importance of Good Roots

# The Importance
of Good Roots

Richard M. Grove

*First Edition*

The Importance of Good Roots
by Richard M. Grove

Layout and Design – Richard M. Grove
Cover Design – Richard M. Grove
Cover Photographs – Richard M. Grove


Typeset in Garamond
Printed and bound in USA

Library and Archives Canada Cataloguing in Publication

Grove, Richard M. (Richard Marvin), 1953-
     The importance of good roots / Richard M. Grove. -- 1st ed.

Short stories and poems.
ISBN 978-1-897475-97-3

     I. Title.

PS8563.R75I46 2013          C818'.54          C2013-901046-7

To my parents,
Marvin and Ruth
for their good roots.

Thank you,
Bruce Kauffman
Jennifer Footman
and Donna Langevin
for your editing and support.

Thank you my darling wife, Kim
for your constant support
in everything that I do.

# Table of Contents

Preface – *p. xiii*

Cemetery Walk – *p. 1*
Orbit of Violence – *p. 2*
Hally's Comet – *p. 3*
The Slivers of Life – *p. 4*
5:20 pm Toronto – *p. 7*
And Never Coming Back – *p. 8*
Woodstock Invation – *p. 11*
The Grey Dog in the Parking Lot
            in the Twilight Zone – *p. 12*
A Journey Into the Dark – *p. 17*
What Could Have Been,
            What Might Have Been – *p. 18*
A Choice Worth Making – *p. 31*
Chill Man – *p. 32*
The Chosen One – *p. 34*
He Was a Hansome Big Old Guy – *p. 37*
Everything is Relative – *p. 33*

The Importance of Good Roots
            Chapter 1 – Only Worth Hangin' – *p. 39*
            Chapter 2 – Don't Let Go of the Pole – *p. 45*
            Chapter 3 – Cut from the Same Cloth – *p. 52*
            Chapter 4 – Cultivate Your Garden – *p. 56*
            Chapter 5 – Mike's Got No Pa – *p. 61*
            Chapter 6 – Naked as a Jay Bird – *p. 66*
            Chapter 7 – The Blur of Time – *p. 70*
            Chapter 8 – Slug in the Sun – *p. 77*

# Preface

*The Importance of Good Roots* is a collection of short stories and poems. The stories are about the ties of family and friends and the roots that tie people together. A not so veiled theme of forgiveness permeates the book.

This collection of short stories has come after my book entitled, *Psycho Babble and the Consternations of Life*, also a collection of short stories and poems though of a different flavour. In *Psycho Babble*, the book ends with a depressing story of no hope. While I loved the writing of that book, *The Importance of Good Roots* has a very different tone and is more about emotional ties. It is about the roots that tie people together. It is about growing to understand motivation that is based in emotion.

One story revolves around a two person, post-funeral conversation about a recently deceased friend and the motivations that propelled his life. The reader is left with the ambiguity of whether or not the deceased character committed suicide. In another vein, the book starts with a one page short story that leaves the reader only with questions about the motivation of a cryptic pre-death farewell conversation. The pivotal story with eponymous title is a story that I am most proud of: a young boy grows up in an abusive relationship with a guardian grandmother in the shadow of his mother's suicide. The story starts and ends with the concept of forgiveness that is linked to personal growth.

This book is the least autobiographical of anything that I have written. *Trapped in Paradise*, is a straight up memoir about my travels in Cuba, as is, *From Cross Hill*. My first collection, *The Family Reunion*, is a fun collection of character vignettes that are often based on autobio-graphical snippets of my life or events I borrowed from family members – it has been described as "Stephen Leacock meets the Waltons". *The Importance of Good Roots* is 99% fiction. I did not come from an abusive family, my mother is still alive and kicking, though I do have a brother named Chris. Perhaps the most autobiographical of any of my books is my first collection of poetry entitled *Beyond Fear and Anger*. Cathartic is the best word to describe that book.

I am delighted that *The Importance of Good Roots* is finally in print. It took me years to weave through the landscape of understanding something about forgiveness and the emotional motivation that lies beneath. The question of just how accurate are our memories is an unanswered sub-current that flows throughout a couple of the stories.

In *The importance of Good Roots*, I explore the idea that forgiveness cannot possibly change the past but it does enlarge the future into possibilities that would never be there without forgiveness. Desmond Tutu said, "Without forgiveness, there is no future". Some of the characters in this collection of short stories explore this notion in different ways. Mahatma Gandhi said, "The weak can never forgive. Forgiveness is the attribute of the strong." One character in particular turns an unexpected corner learning this lesson.

I am thrilled that you have this book in your hands.

Richard M. Grove

# Cemetery Walk

*For Michael (Mack) MacWhirter*

Leaves under November foot
crunch as I meander, camera poised
through a century of listing slabs
pitted white granite,
time-stained grey.

A distant train whistles
reminding me that time
moves on, sometimes too fast,
sometimes as slow as the green
and rust red lichen      clinging,
in humble desperation
some try to slow or stop time
with plastic wreaths, fresh
red roses never fading
inscriptions of love chiseled
but in the end even granite
will melt into time's clutches
turning to dust, heartfelt words
no matter how deeply carved
no matter how deeply felt
will eventually fade
like graying goldenrod forever
past its prime
forgotten.

# Orbit of Violence

You, like Io
in Jupiter's alluring embrace
revolve in orbit
around your captor.
One moment almost out of range
at furthest reaches of your journey
with a lessening pull on you
you are not quite ready to slip
from magnetic charm.

The next moment pulled back
a moth to candle racing
into the arms of singeing embrace.
Wings burned, you are one of many moons
that revolve in yearning attraction
an appeal not worthy of your potential.

Will you ever realize that while in your
non-symmetrical elliptical orbit that you are
nearest your perfect self when furthest
his relentless gravity?

Will you ever realize that your violent
volcanic seething lessens only as you once again
spin to outer reaches
once again almost out of grasp
only to swirl to your endless cycle
of demise in time without end?

# Halley's Comet

Tail trailing 9 million miles
crossing forever night
you are a spectacular sight.
Earth's distant baby cousin
one hundred times removed,
the last time I saw you
I was an infant at thirty-three.
If I see you before I am one-hundred and nine
it may be because I have joined
with you, at one with the solar system.
Maybe my coma of dust and gas will match
your hundreds of thousands of miles of
sun lit glory as we dash around mother sun
in forever orbit.
Our tiny nucleus of ten miles at the head
of our glorious solar-wind-swept tails,
always pushed away from mother,
our tilted elongated orbit
that takes us a billion miles
will let us visit brother Enche
in his bosom suckling orbit
only once in 76 years

# The Slivers of Life

The day was filled with the mundane,
rising rather late to the "Dini Petti Show"
but then again I had had a late night,
      I am not apologizing.
Tiredly moving from one pragmatic,
        sometimes impractical
articulation of life to another I seem numb
      or just unconscious.
The day unfolds to nothing,
      it drains and just disappears.
I sit on the toilet, now late at night,
      4:05 am to be exact.
The dishwasher that I had just loaded whirs
      in the background,
my face pressed into hands, feet cold, naked.
I am fully clothed but I feel stripped,
dispossessed of my own thinking.
The idea of a fragment of wax comes to mind,
you know the tiny pieces
      that you peal up from a candle
or scrape with thumbnail from the tablecloth
      beside a burning candle
those fragments that one can neither wash
      nor even scrub away but
they beg to be picked or poked .
I had gathered such scraps of wax
      only twenty minutes ago
placing them unconsciously into the melted pool
      of a burning candle

but now this act struck me as profound.
I flush, haul up my pants
            as I bound to my computer
to dashed down these two lines.

fragments of wax
slivers of life

Now, this next day those lines don't
            seem all that deep
in fact they feel as trite and as unworthy as numbly
            watching tv at 10 a.m.
At almost 50 years of age I wished
            I could do that to my life,
simply slip slivers of life into my moat of melted wax
            as my flame flickers
sucking fuel from my candle as it gently
            scents the room.


## Continued Dialogue: *

Some days I feel like a wax blob,
no longer associated
with a working candle,
but hardened on some tabletop,
waiting for the fastidious maid of time
to pick or poke me into some crumb filled rag
to be tossed into the garbage.

Hopefully this maid of time will be more like you,
a friend who will think only to reintroduce me
to my process of reliquification
and send me home to my candlepool.

This makes me think of Odo
          on Star Trek – Deep Space Nine
the shape-shifter that is homeless but
               immortal
partly dead inside because he is not
          connected to the Continuum.
Is it enough that my candle gently scent the room?

** Continued Dialogue is from a reply from Eric.
I edited his email reply to my poem and added it
to my poem.  The last stanza is mine.*

# 5:20 pm Toronto

An endless stream of people poured
off the eastbound King street car
at University Ave.
Everyone flushed down the subway stairs
as if into a gutter.

A current of undulating bodies
created an undertow
that no individual could resist.
Bodies coursed to the subway
through underground tributaries
the arteries of the city
bobbing bodies innocently drawn
to their predetermined destinations.

Captured trout in a can
throbbing, not speaking
hardly acknowledging
each other's body-pressed existence
mute to the trauma of vulnerability
numb to pure unquestioned anonymity.

Faces refusing to smile,
stared into the confines of closeness
trying hard to ignore their self denial
buried as deep as humanly possible
in their private knowledge that they
will sooner or later spill
from the urban river
into the comfort of their own pond.

# And Never
# Coming Back

**Hello, Bob here.**

Oh, Frank, how you doin'? What's up?

Yah, I got your email saying you were going away and never coming back.  I figured it was a joke and I just didn't get around to sending a quip reply.

What do you mean you are or you aren't? You are going away and you aren't coming back? What's that mean? Where you going? Surely you are coming back eventually even if only to visit.

No! What do you mean no?

Ok, ok I got it. Your're leaving and you're never coming back. Where are you going? Can I come and see you sometime?

What do you mean, No?! Well eventually. No as in never or no as in you don't know when?

Ok, ok I got it your're leaving and you're never coming back and I can't come to visit you, or at least you hope not for a very long time from now. Email, how about email can I still email you?

No? Oh. Well where are you going that you won't have email?

Ok, ok. You won't have a computer but there are internet cafés. Set up a Yahoo or Hotmail account before you go and I'll email you if or when you get to a computer some time.

No email. Ok, ok no email. Where the hell are you going, the Antarctic with a dog team for the rest of your life or a monastery? Where are you going anyway? Why all the secrecy for frickin' sakes? When are you leaving?

You don't know exactly but you know you are going soon and you can't tell me where and I can't email you? Sounds pretty bloody cryptic to me. If you change your mind email me and…

Ok, ok no email but what the hell man? I've known you for 28 years and you're just dropping off the face of the earth and you can't tell me anything. Trouble, are you in some sort of trouble? Maybe I can help. What's the problem? Money, I'll send you some money, how much do you need? Money makes all problems disapear.

You don't need any money were you're going? No email, no money, I presume no snail mail or phone. Where are you going Shangri-La? If you don't need money and you can't have email you might as well be dead man. Come on, man, give me a hint.

I love you too man! What's with all of the sappy I love you stuff anyway?

## Woodstock Invation

After a long arduous desk-hunched day
my darling wife beckoned me
for a -17oC wind whistling walk
to clear the frazzled monitor-flickered brain.
South towards the lake, wind pelted,
head hunched, frosted glasses.
A half mile down the road
we see a distant black undulating V
stitching grey quiet sky,
fifty Canadian Geese slowly swelling
towards us. The discord of dissonant honking
gradually filled the air.

Thrilled
we stood, back to wind and watched
V after weaving V arrive landing
by the hundreds. Descending,
content in their now two-thousand
billowing, blasting frenzy, foraging
in snowless corn-stubbled field. It struck me
that this was their Woodstock invasion
gathering on mass for a union of sorts
mulling, communing
guided by primeval callings.

# The Grey Dog in the Parking Lot in the Twilight Zone

**I darted from my tv-flickering-sofa-dinner slumber,** jumped into clean clothes and slumped into my car. I am rag tired as usual but if I hurry I can still make the 90-minute drive north to a poetry reading in the tiny town of Norwood, Ontario.

I got to the reading venue in plenty of time before the MC introduced the first reader. The store where the reading was taking place was called "The Cat Sass" – an obvious joke on the phrase "The Cat's Ass".

As I pulled into the dog-lazy town I stopped and leaned out the car window towards a gaggle of teenagers slumped over a garbage can puffing on a joint. With careful pronunciation I asked if they knew where the Cat Sass was. My request for directions was met with hilarious cackles and gesticulations. "Oh fuck yah man, the fuckin' Cat's Ass is just around the corner man. Fuckin' cool place man, you can't miss it." Thirty seconds later I was prancing into a very cool store front, coffee shop, come music store, filled with funky stuff. I bought a coffee – decaf – and a fab-fat muffin. After a quick chit chat with a few friends I settled in for the readings for which I almost fell asleep – a reflection of how tired I was not on the quality of the readings. Half way through I stood at the back of the store with no wall to rest on so my mind would be alert to the authors' contributions.

After the readings and more pleasantries exchanged I

headed home tracing my circuitous country route, driving through the tunnel of black, silver headlights piercing the now ebony wall. I got to the small town of Hastings where I needed to turn and change from highways #45 to #25. After the turn I drove for 30 minutes before I realized that I had taken the wrong spoke in the convoluted junction. No problem I thought, I will just turn right instead of going all the way back to my misguided turn. I turned onto a pitch dark road where not even a cow's silver eyes were present to dart me in the right direction. Oh finally lights in the distance. I must be close to home.

I took another turn onto another well marked but desolate road. Strange, very strange, it was the #7 highway. My two choices were, west to Toronto or east to Ottawa. Toronto I knew was wrong so east I chose. 40 minutes later I arrived in Norwood, can you believe it, right back at exactly the town from where I had departed. How on earth is that possible?!!!!!!!!!!

I looked at my map and with no hesitation I headed back out of the now sleeping town of Norwood. A mangy grey-haired dog sat in the parking lot of a slumbering Coffee Time store front that I had driven past an hour ago. The dog sat on his left haunch gazing at the flickering street lights. Most assuredly he did not notice the bewildered glaze that veiled my tired eyes as I slowly, very cautiously drove out of town for the second time.

A silly smirk drained from my tired squinting face. Ok finally there is Hastings again where I must have made my fatal turnabout mistake. A small sign said highway #45 turn right. So, there is no bloody way I am going to make that mistake and follow 45 again. With a sense of school boy pride I snubbed the turn and continued straight looking for highway #25 south.

Pride has a way of biting you in the cat's ass if you are not careful. Three minutes later I realized that I was not on the right path after all. Once again the town of Hastings foiled my return home. I pulled into the parking lot of Smith and Smith Funeral Home to make a quick recalculation. With a tentative smile I zipped through the dead town and put the pedal to the metal. What I did not realize was that I was driving in the "Twilight Zone". Fifteen long minutes later, there ahead of me was the Norwood neon flickered grey dog. How on earth is that possible?!!!!!!!!!!!

I pulled in beside my grey-haired buddy that still sat basking in star light to gather my senses. The map light revealed that I had simply traveled back through the same tunnel of doom after leaving Smith and Smith's. It would appear that all wrong turns lead back to the cat's ass and the neon flickered grey dog. I shut my eyes for ten minutes, composed myself and without even an ounce of confidence I headed once again into the void.

When I arrived at the infamous Hastings intersection for the third time I sat refusing to make a turn. I sat and read the sign that said #45. I read the sign that said #2 and the arrow that pointed to #10. I consulted my map again and again. At 3 miles an hour I coasted through the red blinking intersection. I coasted towards the #45 against all instinct. I coasted past the familiar Home Hardware store. I gently, slowly, glided past the church on the right, the municipal building on the left and finally there it was the arrow under the #25 south sign. I tentatively, ever so slowly drifted to the left of the fork in the road past the monument, over the bridge. I floated for five minutes refusing to put my foot on the gas until I was confident that I was finally out of the Twilight Zone and heading in the right direction. Thirty-minutes later I was pulling into the security of my gravel Wicklow driveway. For just a moment, a millisecond, I swear I saw the grey-haired dog sitting on his haunch waiting for me. A raccoon lumbered out of the beams of my car lights. I was home.

# A Journey Into the Dark

My little brother Christopher
held my hand firm
in the now cool evening
of September.
"Don't be a sissy boy." I said.
"Come.
Let me show you the stars."

We walked away from the bright lights
of the front porch
into the dark
toward the open sky.
Silver stripes of dew painted
our legs as we walked
through the uncut grass
at the edge of the lawn
down into the distant hay field
north past the lane.

This was territory little Christopher
had not yet ventured into
during the day
let alone at night.
I was the brave 13 year old big brother,
he was 9 years younger
clinging close to my side
into the dark to see the brilliant sky
in a way that had not yet
been revealed to him.

# What Could Have Been What Might Have Been

**Two men sit in an upscale, Toronto café.** The armchairs are large, rich green and plush.  They sit close to the back of the café away from the glare of the afternoon light that spills through the large windows facing the street. Traffic noise, seeps a sad song of busy to the back of the restaurant where they slump.

Mark is a handsome man, in a polished sort of way, dressed in a brown, obviously high end pinstripe, three-piece suit.  Gold cufflinks peer out from under the gold buttoned suit cuffs. His greying hair is slicked back into perfection.

Bob is a ruggedly handsome man with a chiseled, suntanned face. He is dressed in black jeans, stiffly new, with a white shirt, a narrow black leather tie from the 70's and a black leather bomber jacket. His tie is pulled loose and the top button of his shirt is undone.

Both men wear the same joyless, somber look on their freshly shaven faces.

"Miss, if I wanted 'Café a la Dishwater' I would have gone down the street to Joe's greasy spoon. At least you get what you pay for there." Mark leans forward from an almost reclined position, wipes the foam from his upper lip with his handkerchief and pushes his frothing, cinnamon-sprinkled bowl of latté towards the waitress. "What the heck do you call this? Bring me another one, make sure it's made right and by the way, why I should have to say 'make sure it's hot' is beyond me and please don't take all day about it."

Bob slumps further into his chair rolling his eyes. "Mark, take it easy on the gal. I know you're a regular in this fancy joint but..."

The waitress silently whisks the bowl from the table. Without a word she walks away.

"Since when did you get so high and mighty, Mr. Three-piece-pin-striped-suit? I've known you for over 25 years and you didn't used to talk to people like that."

Holding the palm of his left hand up to Bob's face, Mark flips open his cell phone and growls, "Yah, what is it now?"

Bob sits in silence, patiently waiting for Mark to return to the conversation.

"Sorry about that guy. I can't be away from the office for more than two seconds before some idiot calls and I have to put out one fire or another. Bob, what were you saying you do these days? Where are you living now?"

"I'm living in BC. Have been for three years now. Don't you remember I sent you a Christmas card with a picture of my land before I started building? I do a little of this and a bit of that. Whatever brings in some cash but mostly carpentry work, mostly small stuff, decks and garages and stuff like that."

"So you're a contractor now. Congratulations."

"No way, it's just me doing odd jobs I can mostly do on my own or with a buddy helping.  I'm building my own place up near Edgemont in the hills looking down to the ocean. I got the land cheap from my uncle and have mostly been using timbers from the land to. You should fly out to see the place when I'm done. It's coming along real nice now. It's a post and beam, stack log house with walls that are 18 inches thick, with a stone passive solar collector on the south wall, a compost toilet, a solar generator system, an energy efficient wood stove..."

Mark shuffles in his chair and swats the air towards Bob. "Hey, slow down Bob, take a breath man. I know you're excited about your house but weren't you working on the plans for a log cabin 20 years ago? It's about time you got off your ass and finally built it. I knew you would. Better late than neveer.  I remember you tried to get Jimmy, Billy and me to buy in on some land somewhere north of Toronto near Georgian Bay so you could build a log cabin and sell it and make a killing.  I remember I put the kibosh on the deal because it would have been too risky. I still think it would have been too risky.  It would have tied up all of our cash for too long. Get in and out is how you make money in real estate. Sell and make a killing. If we had have bought that little bungalow in Etobicoke and flipped it, we could have made some decent coin.  A bit of paint, cut the grass and flip it. Bob, you wanted us to buy into a tree-hugging pipe dream, not make an investment."

"Yah, yah, money, profit, return on investment, always

has to fit in your equation. Always flippin' did.  If it wasn't going to make fast money you didn't want anything to do with it.  Hell, even Billy was ready to sink his hard-earned tree planting money into that property with me. He was the first one in, then Jim, but we couldn't swing it without you coming in so we canned the project and shelved the dream.  Even though it's all so long ago, I can still see it in my mind's eye. It was just one concession road south of a pretty little town called Lafontaine, an hour and a half from the top of Toronto – 26 beautiful acres and had a pretty little year-round brook. It was gorgeous, calm and quiet and here's the thing... affordable. We could have got it for fifty-five grand or maybe less. All we had to do was bulldoze a laneway in and we could have started building right from the trees on the property."

"Bob, Bob shut up, you are so full of crap you're starting to stink. We've heard it all before a thousand times.  Twenty years hasn't changed a thing. That 26 acres of, so called, idyllic land was full of nothing but scrub brush, hardly worth cutting even for firewood and where the heck were you planning on sticking your heavenly log house anyway?  Most of the property was wet all year round.  Hell, the only small patch that was dry and had any sun reach the ground Billy wanted to grow pot on it."

"Hey man, you don't have to rip into me.  When did you get to be such a hard nut?"

Mark waves the back of his hand at Bob as if shooing a fly. "Don't try to shut me up after you just ran on like a trip hammer about me not wanting to invest twenty years ago. I haven't seen you for almost three years and you start jabbering on about the great lost investment opportunity. I'm going to say this one last time; I didn't really want to go to jail for growing pot and I didn't want to stick around 'til I was sixty to see a return on my investment. Twenty years and you are still babbling on about how "I" personally sabotaged your dreams. Grow up man. What would you be doing now if I did come in with you on that deal?  You'd still be doing nothing, absolutely nothing. Zippo would be different so get over it and let's finally move on for Christ sakes!"

"Holy crappers Mark, let's cool it. We're both a bit edgy considering what just brought us here after all this time.  I'm pretty flipped out about Billy being dead too. Heck Billy was like a brother to both of us.  As Billy would have said, 'Time to chill man.'"

"Well one thing for sure, Billy would have tried growing pot on the land, no doubt.  Do you remember when he scored some weed seed and sprouted about 100 plants right in our living room?  I was so nervous we were going to get caught I demanded he get rid of them. He kept one growing in our hall closet with a uv light and the rest he just planted down in the ravine and out at my father's cottage beside the farmer's field."

"Mark, you're so crazy.  He didn't have 100 plants. It was more like 10 and he took only one out to your dad's cottage. Your dad was such a pot head he grew it, in a planter, on his deck . Every time we went out the plant was smaller and smaller.  He was smoking it all right."

Mark heaves himself forward, loosens his tie and opens his collar. He sighs as he starts to speak in a firm staccato voice. "My dad... was not... a pot head. He smoked a bit of weed once in college but swore he never inhaled."

Bob laughed outloud. "Yah I know He didn't smoke pot with Bill Clinton at the same party he didn't inhale.

"Billy took that pot plant and put it on my dad's deck and told him it was a Mediterranean medicinal herb that was poisonous if not properly mixed with other herbs. If anybody was a pot head it was Billy. I don't mean to bad mouth Billy, he was our buddy, hell our brother. I'm sorry he's dead but the damned plant didn't even last the summer before Billy smoked it stock and all. He couldn't even wait 'til it was full grown for Pete's sake."

Bob leans forward and pushes Mark on the shoulder. "Mark, you just thought it as a money plant. You told Billy he should let it mature and harvest the leaves and sell them but you know Billy, he wanted everything now. Now or never. His mom always said, when he was a boy, he wanted to eat his dessert first. I figure Billy would still be with us today if he could've just slowed down and waited for what he wanted but no he had to go out in the canoe even though there was a storm brewing. Anyone else would have waited until the storm passed or 'til the next day but not good old Billy Boy. Heck, he was't even that great of a canoer."

"He had to go right then and there. Now, now, now, never soon or later. I guess the bloody pot and the alcohol they found in his system didn't help in the logic department. Billy was a good guy though. Not too smart sometimes but a good guy; I'll miss him for sure. He might have been impulsive but sometimes it worked for him. Do you remember the time we all biked over to the quarry? I think we must have biked over because no one had their licence back then. It was a hot day in August before school started and we took a pack of hot dogs and matches to make lunch."

Bob reaches across the table towards Mark, almost spilling his coffee and grabs at his shirt, laughs and pushes him away. "We all chipped in to buy hot dogs but you stole them frozen from your mom instead of buying them. Come to think of it you still owe me the fifteen cents that I gave you for my share.

"It's amazing. I remember just like it was yesterday, Bob continued. We were walking our bikes through the underbrush ducking the low branches and watching that we didn't step in any poison ivy that lined the path. All of a sudden we hear this yelling and screaming so we ran further up the path to the edge of the cliff. By the time we got there it was too late, there was a kid lying face down in the water and his canoe was overturned about twenty feet away drifting to shore. We all hesitated, do you remember. But not Billy. It was like he had a part in a movie and he knew exactly what he had to do before he did it. He dropped his bike and took a running dive off the cliff, swam over to the kid and saved his life."

Mark settled back in his chair, "Yeah I know what you

mean, there was no hesitation. As soon as he saw the kid he took off running and dove off the cliff. He was the one that jumped in not us. We carefully tiptoed through the poison ivy and made our way down the path to the edge of the water.  By the time we got down there Billy was already pumping on the kid's chest and doing mouth to mouth. He was a frickin' hero.  He brought him back to life for sure.  He would have been a goner if it hadn't been for Billy. He was the one that jumped in after that kid, not any of us."

Mark squirms in his seat, "I was going to jump in. I would've jumped in if Billy hadn't. Hell any one of us would have jumped in to save the kid."

"Maybe" said Bob, "but I guess the point is that it was Billy. Billy did it and didn't hesitate.  That's the thing. You have to admire him for that.  It's not what could have been or what might have been, it's actually what happened that counts."

"It's ironic, a stoner like Billy saved the kid's life and then years later he drowns in a stupid canoeing accident."

Bob shrugs, "It's more than just ironic man, it's sad."

Mark reaches in his pocket for his hankerchief and wipes his eyes, "The person I feel saddest for is Jenny.  For all of the impulsive things Billy did he could never commit to Jenny.  She patiently hung around living with him for years wishing they would get married and have kids. Right up to the end she wished they were married. Did you hear her telling some people at the funeral that she was his wife?"

"Yah, kind of weird, I was thinking that she might just pack up and move on but now that he's dead she doesn't have to, she can just be his widow.  It's weird that she finally gets to be his wife only because he died. He found the ultimate excuse not to get married and he ends up having a wife through his death.  If it wasn't so weird it would be funny. It's the kind of thing they write movies about."

Mark leans forward, looks over his shoulder in the direction of the waitress at the counter serving someone else.  He fusses in his chair. "Where the hell's my latté anyway? What the hell's she doing chatting that guy up while my latté is sitting there getting cold."

He looks directly at Bob. "Dead is a pretty permanent excuse not to get married.  Do you think that we make decisions subconsciously like that? If we do then I guess way down deep he thought it was better to be dead than commit or change."

Bob smirks and nods at Mark. "I guess you pissed the waitress off. You're at the end of the line now buddy. I learned a long time ago from my mother that tone of voice is everything, man. I'll bet she's ticked and you aren't getting your latté without kissin' her butt."  He leans forward and pulls his cup closer. "Billy's dead, man, and you're more worried about your stupid cup of coffee than anything. What's with you? Man, you would have to have a lot of fear in your life to choose death over just about anything else. Do you think that someone would...."

Without letting Bob finish, Mark interrupts, "I miss

Billy but why do you think he was stoned all the time or taking so many stupid risks? If my psych 101 class at university taught me anything it was that impulsive risk-taking behaviour like heading into a storm in a canoe, stoned, without a life jacket, without telling anyone, was the classic sign of a disturbed mind. It smacks of suicide to me."

"Suicide, do you really think it was suicide?"

Mark looks over his shoulder at the waitress and mumbles a profanity under his breath. "Remember the time we all went out to Rockwood Conservation area? We drove out late one night in Jimmy's dad's car, the old brown Dodge. We stripped off our clothes, tucked them under our arms and ran through the park naked. When we got to the river Bill dove head first off the waterfall and pretended that he was drowning. We were all stoned but Billy, the silly bastard, was the only one that dove head first off the falls, scared the crap out of all of us. Now that was suicidal if anything is."

"It was different than that, man, I remember everyone jumped off the falls except you Mark. Everyone but you. You were the only one that chickened out. Billy was the only one that dove head first, the rest of us, except for you, jumped."

Mark fidgetted, "Yah and what's your point idiot?"

"Don't you remember we were down in the river screaming – 'Billy's dead, Billy's dead. He cracked his head on the rocks and he's dead.' You came running down the hill and splashed your way in to the deep part of the river.

By the time you got there we were gone.  We were up the other side and stole your clothes and ran into the park leaving you in the dark." Bob nods towards the front of the café. "Hey, here comes your coffee.  Take it from the master of diplomacy, just say 'thank you miss' and then shut your mouth."

Mark sneers.

"Finally, I came out to get you because you were just about bawling.  Don't you remember I had to slug Billy to get your clothes back?  He always wanted to push it just a bit further than the rest of us."

"Thank you, miss."

"Mark... Now just shut up, don't say another word to her." Bob looks down at his own drink and then up at Mark. "Well eventually we got back to the car and Billy wouldn't get in.  He was howling like a coyote and hollering at us, calling us all a bunch of whimps. Finally we drove away without him."

Mark takes a long satisfied sip of his cappuccino. "Yah and we came back a few minutes later.  There he was in the dark still sitting naked on a stump covered in mosquitoes. The only thing he said when we pulled up to get him was he figured it would take us longer to come back for him than it did.

"He called us wimps all the way home. He called me a wimp the last time I saw him.  The only way to shut him up and get him to put his clothes back on was when we pulled into Harvey's for a burger and we left him in the car."

Mark sits back hard in his chair. "So who is the wimp now? Silly bastard. You could dive off a waterfall in the dark, you could save a kid's life but you couldn't figure out that it wasn't safe to go canoeing, or could you? Silly bastard."

"Maybe we just gotta accept him for who he was. We'll have to do a proper toast to Billy Boy later with a beer at the Rex but for now coffee will have to do. Here's to the silly bastard and all the times we had together. I guess its not a matter of what could have been or might have been."

They both raised their coffees, clinked them together over the centre of the low table and slumped heavy back into their chairs. They sat ponderously quiet for the longest time.

# A Choice Worth Making

Shall we merely weather the storm,
survive the cauldron of these
tumultuous times
with the girding of loin
and shielding of breast?
Shall we clench our teeth
and muscle under
in personal triumph
with persistence,
the true grit of endurance
or shall we glide above
the seeming assault
like a sail on storm's crest
joyously riding the tempest
to the victory of peace
unsullied by the stain
of revenge or retaliation,
untouched or moved by
trepidation or terror
by riding on the fearless
wing of the Divine's protection
that when clung to
will govern, guard and guide us
through certain harmony?

# Chill Man

**"Hey man don't be an old fussy fart** just cuz you can't stand not knowing. I read once that when we're faced with a challenge or tough kind of thing that we aren't able to change then the real challenge is to change ourselves and not be screwed up about it."

"You stupid arss, who the hell told you such a stupid thing? You been reading the scratchings in the toilet stall again? Stupid Weirdo. You sure as hell never read it in no Playboy."

"Bugger off. I can't remember where I read it. It is from some old dead guy I guess. I probably read it in *Reader's Digest* or some other magazine. I don't really know what it means but it sounds deep. It kinda makes sense to me though. I was thinking about it the other night when I couldn't sleep. If you can't change a situation there is no point in fussin' over it and drivin' yourself crazy. Just chill out and be calm. I think that's what he must have meant by change yourself. Change your attitude.

"It's like you man, you don't know if you're going to loose your job or not and you're flippin' out about it. You've been working at the same machine at the steel plant for how many years? You're so used to it by now that you can't change without you fussin' an' worryin' like an old monkey that might have his banana taken away from him and here he is sittin' in a banana tree."

# The Chosen One

Little do you know
that you are the chosen one
as you calmly chomp your way
from one green shady patch
under a giant Cedar tree to another
in the heat of a Cuban day.

You are the chosen one.
Round belly, soft velvet floppy ears,
a wisp of a grey beard that twitches
as you mindlessly stop and munch.

You are the chosen one.
Carefree, no concept of past or future.
Only one moment of now
strung into eternity.

You are the chosen one.
Hung by hind cloven hooves
to face a dusty patch of red
stained earth,
left to sway gently.

You are the chosen one.
The pendulum of life
ticking
       life / death,
       life / death,
Paralyzed,
       motionless,
           now still.

You are the chosen one.
Life drains from
your still pulsing neck
into dinted tin pan
splashed to thin black pigs.
Hot life to squeals of delight.

You are the chosen one.
Not a single bray
will you utter in protest.
Not a single plea
or frantic flailing,
mesmerized by your duty
to succumb.

You are the chosen one.
Skinned, butchered, cooked,
served over a bountiful
bonding table of friendship.

You are the chosen one.
Your sacrifice fills the bellies
and the hearts of ten
with much left over.
You the chosen one
will live forever hanging
in this moment of gratitude.

# He Was a Handsome Big Old Guy

A big old moth came fluttering frantically,
dive bombing through the pitch dark
of a moonless night.
dazed by the flicker of our single candle,
crashing crazily,
no purpose,
objective unknown.

Two large dime size silver eyes painted
adorn the back of his soft matt-grey wings.

He's a handsome big old guy,
when he is standing still that is,
otherwise he is an undulating blur
of random indecision.

Then with a plunge,
a hiss,
he's a blaze of magnificence
then a speck of char bobbing
in the pool of melted wax
at the base of the flame.

# The Importance of Good Roots

*The past casts a sometime heavy mist over the present. It seeps deep to the roots of being and in every case feeds the future.*

Chapter 1

# *Only Worth Hangin'*

*Sunlight slants through perfect, tiny, yellow leaves of a gigantic maple to cool virgin grass flowing across outstretched legs. Clouds wander gracefully from the northeast over spring-filled hills. Toe taps to a song that swims through mind like a leaf gliding on glistening ripples of a gentle creek. Life flows effortlessly, snaglessly to a sea unknown. It is early May.*

**"Mike, Mike, over here."**

"Sorry I'm late, man. My Grams made me stack some of next winter's firewood against the wall of the back kitchen. I never stacked so much so fast and then she had me rake up the bark bits and then feed the rabbits. If it weren't a school day she would a' had me doin' something else and I never would a' made it. You been here long?"

"I've been here for hours. I snuck out before it even got light. My Dad gets up early so I figured I had better get up and feed the chickens before he gave me something more to do."

Mike kicked Chris's foot to make him move over to share the rock and lay in the cool grass beside him. He toed off his shoes, no socks and grumbled, "These dang things are supposed to be my new shoes. Grams got them for free off a' one of her friends. Grams said I'll grow into them. Maybe by the time I'm twenty I figure and they'll be worn out by then. He slid down and put his head on the rock beside Chris.

"Mike, we are going to get in trouble for skippin' school. My sister wouldn't write us a note this time. She jabbered on about us going to 'H – E

— Double Hockey Sticks' and she wasn't planning on joining us. She said she is going to tell Mr. Finlan that she has been writing all of those notes for us. She said she is going to go and confess to Father Horner as soon as she can make it to church so God doesn't punish her too."

Mike shuffled in the grass and sat up. "I might be goin' to hell, man, but not you. You've been going to church since you was born. My Grams never made me go. Not even once. Grams says there's no hope for me. I just try to stay out of trouble so as I don't get no beatin'. I figure hell's not worse than living with Grams, besides skippin' school ain't goin' to get you into hell. You gotta murder someone or steal something big to go to hell. You don't go to hell for skippin' school."

Mike reached forward and rubbed his sore feet. "Do you gotta wear shoes in hell?"

"Maybe you just go naked, who knows."

"There's no girls in hell any way so who knows. The one good thing about goin' to hell is that my Grams won't be there unless maybe there is a separate hell for women. Hell I don't know. I guess no one knows for sure."

"I figure we just turn to worm food anyway so it doesn't much matter. My Mom has been taking my sister and me to church since forever but my Dad never goes. He says God is all around us and he doesn't need any church to pray. I figure my Dad just doesn't like to shave till the afternoon on Sundays. I go just to make my Mom happy."

Mike and Chris laid with their heads on the cold rock watching the clouds roll by and the sun climbing higher in the sky.

"Mike, what did you want to meet down here by the creek for any way and why did you want me to bring matches? I had to sneak them from the kitchen drawer." Chris laughed out loud and smacked Mike on the side. He said, "I sure hope I don't go to hell for stealing penny matches."

Mike pulled a crumpled piece of paper out of his pocket. "This is why. You remember when I was over to your place a few weeks ago and we was watchin' Oprah and they was talking about fogivin' people and there was this lady that forgave a man who murdered her son and there was another who forgave this man for rapin' her when she was just a little girl and she wrote him a letter forgivin' him and she put it in the river and she said it washed out to the ocean and she was healed of grief and it made her life better? Well, I got to thinkin' about Grams and thought I maybe should write her a letter and put it in the creek only thing is that I want to turn it into a paper boat and set it on fire. We are too far from the ocean here so I figure I will put it up in smoke. If nothin' else it will be fun to watch. First I think I gotta read it out loud or something.

*Dear Grams:*

*I'm sorry I wasn't particular tight with you when I was growin' up. I am sorry that by the time I was ten you thought I was only worth hangin'. I'm sorry that I had to live with you when Ma died and be in your way and all. Maybe if you had hung with me, even just a little, when I was younger I might 'ave turned out more to your likin'. I remember thinking that your house was like a train station, people comin' and goin' all the time. You hugged everyone that come through your front door. Every time you hugged someone and it wasn't me I hated you even more. Marylou used to hug me and make sure I had something to eat an' she weren't even family. Even Bob, your repair guy, treated me good. He gave me a jack knife once and taught me how to skin a rabbit. Do you remember that one time when Mr. Barker, gave me a cuff up the side of the head just for me bein' me? He made me cry right in front of you and what did you do? Nothin'! Nothin' at all. You would have thought you might have at least pretended to care and give me a hug but you just gave me no mind and pushed me away as you walked off with that old Mr. Barker. I hated you for that and I hated Mr. Barker, the fat old bastard, even more. His pants were always hangin' low so as you could see his bum crack and he farted when he walked; I couldn't figure why you hung with him instead of me. It wasn't till about last year, when I lost my boyhood to your friend, that old gal, what was her name, she had big boobs and a smile that made me shiver; I finally figured out you must have been runnin' a whore house. A whore house, for God sakes Grams and Mr. Barker was your own personal customer. I sure hope that the old fart paid you plenty. Oprah says I gotta learn to forgive you Grams. Writin' ain't my thing so I'm not going to list all of the things that you done to me since Ma died. I forgive you for thinkin' I was dirt and just worth hangin' an' oh I forgive you for all that you done to me.*

*Your Grandson, Michael.*

"Chris, show me how to make it into a paper boat. I'll put it in the creek and light it on fire and let it float away. What do you think?

"I think you are nuts man but I know how to fold paper into boats, give it here. Me and my Dad used to take the Sunday comics after he read them to me and make boats and put them in the pond beside the barn. Here's the matches. Do you want to say anything more before you light it up?"

With silence a match was brought to life, the paper letter boat was lit by Mike and gently placed into the creek. Smoke streamed up for a flicker of eternity vanishing gracefully into the spring air without leaving a trace, ashes fell, with a hiss, into the creek's undulations. The ceremony was over almost before it started. With unusual ponderance the boys stood there wondering about the significance of this transcendent event.

Chapter 2

# Don't Let Go of the Pole

*June is a marvellous time of year. Trees have transformed and are filled with dark green leaves and birds are finished nesting. Fledglings are making their courageous way; the spring air is warm and filled with promise but sometimes one needs to look back to the harsh winter and even beyond, before one can fully enjoy the coming summer. It's a fabulous journey and if one is going to pole one's way across the clear pond, from time to time, one gets the pole stuck in the mud and stirs up a lot of crap. Just don't ever let go of the pole.*

**On this day, in this corner of the country,** the air is sick with sadness. Somehow it feels like a waste of good sunshine. It should be surging with rain to match the mood in the cemetery but God had already punished the Reilly family enough with the dying of Katharine. It was a modern secular style funeral, perhaps better described as a memorial service or a remembrance. Perhaps, not so strangely, there was no mention of God, no reference what so ever. Lots of people stood and said nice things about Katharine. One person reminded everyone that she loved animals and was always rescuing cats and dogs from certain death. A cat half frozen, wet and perilously thin, a dog, Weasel, was just a pup, an ugly mutt that Katharine found skinny, hovering at death's door. She said he weaselled his way out of destiny's grip and into her heart. She brought him home and diligently hunted for the owner while she nursed him back to health. Despite protests from Ma Reilly, Weasel became part of the family.

Someone told a touching story about Katharine giving away her coat to a girl at school that had none. Someone else said she was always taking an extra apple or sandwich for lunch to give away; if she didn't have extra she would go without. One after another, family and friends, stood to tell their stories but the one thing that no one told about was her sadness and pain. It was a prevalent pain that filled the cracks between moments that the rest of the world relaxed in. If it had not been for that pain she would still be alive today.

The family gathered for the first time in years. Mostly everyone had been married or moved away so there had not been the excuse for a family gathering in a long time. As for a family reunion, well, the family was just not all that close. Someone asked if there had ever been a gathering of the clan the size of this funeral; no one could remember when, if ever. The freshness of June wafted gently in the trees. Numb banality hung like heavy humidity on a hot August afternoon. Everyone shuffled slowly to their final goodbye.

*  *  *

Chris and Mike sat out in the middle of the pond on their raft. It was a still day with not even a slight bit of a breeze. "What did you let go of the pole for you idiot?"

"It got stuck in the mud you double idiot."

"Now how are we gunna get back to shore."

"The water's too cold to swim and I gotta keep my clothes clean on account of my mom said we got company comin' over later."

"Even though it's pecker bitin' cold I can swim it. I haven't been dressed up for company since my Ma died almost three weeks ago. I wore grey pants that were a bit too big. Marylou stapled up the pant legs so they were the right length and loaned me a tie from one of her boyfriend."

"My mom and dad went to the funeral but they said that I was too young to go. I have never been to a funeral before. What was it like?"

"I ain't never told anyone about Ma's funeral before. Even though I just wanted to pretend it never happened, I remember it like it was yesterday. For the longest time I just kinda shut most of it out. I remember that Grams was all dressed up in black and could hardly walk for the grief. Old man Barker and my Uncle James, Ma's older brother, stood on each sides of her as she moved slow-like towards the coffin. I remember clear as a bell it hovering over the perfect crisp hole surrounded by green indoor/outdoor carpet; the plastic kind, the same kind as we had in our back porch. It was kinda clean and perfect. Usually you think of ashes to ashes, earth to earth like in the movies but they didn't say anything like that and the pile of earth was all covered up so as you couldn't see it.

"Grams was in awful pain. I remember her moaning as she tried to talk, 'God took my only daughter. How could God do such a thing to me?' I thought it was awful strange her sayin' how could God do such a thing to her. Did God do something to her? All I could figure is that it was my

Ma that was dead and what did God have to do with anything?

"It was a mighty sad time. Grams couldn't even stand to look at me. I remember she told me to stop clingin' to her side and even told old man Barker to take me away from her. At that time I was mighty hurt but it was one of those things that Marylou told me to put behind me. "You've got too much pain already Mikie, just forget about the little stuff. There's no point in hangin' on to hurts. Just let them go." She would rub my head, give me a kind squeeze and tuck in my shirt.

"All I remember was the pain Gram was in and her sayin' that she could only see my Ma's face in mine and she couldn't bear to look at me. I didn't want to be responsible for her bein' in no pain so I just tried to keep outa sight. She kept sayin', "Don't tell me no more that you want your Ma. She's gone boy, gone and we can't help that; you have to be tough. Ted, take him away from me.""

*　*　*

Days turned to weeks, to months, to years and nothing changed with the mood in Ma Reilly's house. Love slowly drained from every corner like the setting sun. . . slowly, inevitably. Ted Barker's frequent visits were met with welcome anticipation. He always brought a bottle; he always brought friends and he always disappeared into her bedroom. He soothed the pain of her broken heart the only way he knew how. The secret of Katharine's suicide was a terrible burden to carry all alone. For Ma Reilly it was a secret that she would carry to her grave. To her knowledge nobody but nobody knew the truth about Katharine's death.

* * *

"Mikie. Where have you been? It's the third time this week you have been late gettin' home from School. What about those pigs? They can't feed themselves. I'll have Ted give you another lickin' if you're late feedin' them one more time. Between you skipping school and stealing at the corner store, I'm fed up. If you ask me you're only worth hangin'."

Mike squeezed past old man Barker who purposefully blocked the door just to make his life a little bit more miserable. He was a husky man, most would say fat. Like a bulldog he had no neck, great floppy jowls hung over his collar. He had a thinly cropped beard and he walked flat footed like he was carrying a stack of bricks on each shoulder.

Under his breath Mike mumbled, "Fat old bastard, what are you doin' here all the time anyway? It's like a train station you bringin' your friends and strangers over two or three times a day and always using my bedroom. Feed the pigs; bring in some firewood; cut the grass. You sure turned into some old bat. One day I'm gunna take off an' never come back. Then they will wish they treated me different, bastard."

To Mike's surprise he kicked weasel in passing and let the screen door slam behind me.  "I wish my Ma was still alive. She'd take me away from here for sure."

Chapter 3

# *Cut from the Same Cloth*

*The smell of pride lingers in the long school corridors. Polished floors shine; the squeal of sneakers echoes against metal lockers like the refrain from a cheap violin. Long shadows murmur teenage secrets; the growing pains and joys of life fill every crack and cranny. Nothing is hidden from these hallowed halls; past and present linger as one. They whisper their secrets to no one but time.*

**Chris gave Mike a jab in the shoulder** and then put his arm around his neck as he dragged him towards math class. The school hallway was bustling with last-minute kids rushing to class. The bell had already rung, they were late . . . again.

"Mike, where have you been? I had to take the flack for both of us for us skippin' school yesterday. Old man Finlan flipped when we didn't show up. We missed a math test. He says that there is no way that you can pass the year and I'm borderline. My mom and dad said I can't hang with you any more on account of you being a bad influence. We gotta cool it for a while or they will move me into another class away from you."

"I can't help it if I'm late. Grams is always givin' me more chores to do. This morning I had to..."

"Shut up about your chores, man. We all have chores to do." Before Mike could finish, Chris dragged him into class. They tip toed to their seats thinking that they might not be noticed.

* * *

The bell rang and clatter ensued. Everyone dashed towards the door to leave for the day. Mr. Finlan bellowed, "Chapter thirteen for tomorrow, . . . Chris and Mike stick around." He slowly marched over to their desks and stood over both of the boys the way one glares at a puppy that has chewed your slippers or pooped on the carpet.

Arms crossed over his chest, looking over the rim of his glasses he scowled. "What am I going to do with you two boys? Mr. Reilly, you have some explaining to do about missing class and the test yesterday. Here we are almost at the end of the year and you are both about to fail. Chris, what is your excuse? You have a good home and parents that care. You're smart but lazy, lazy as a turtle sitting on a log in the sun.

"Mike, you are as bad as your mother ever was. No one could get her to work no matter what. You were both cut from the same bolt. You tell me, am I supposed to just give up on you both? Are you worth my investment? Are you worth anyone's time? I'll work with you both if you want to pull up your socks and make the grade but you have to do the work. If you quit on yourself then you aren't worth me wasting my time. What's it going to be?

"Chris, I talked to your parents last night and I know they are going to make sure you put in the time. No more trips to the pond after school for you young men. Mike, your grandmother says she washes her hands of you. It's up to you, Mike. Open your books to chapter twelve. Finish yesterday's homework and I'll be back in a few minutes to make sure you are working. We will talk about the test make up when I get back."

"Oh man, my Grams is gunna be pissed when I get home. If I don't feed those pigs before Grams finds out I'll be in trouble. If old man Barker is there I ain't going in. Grams will have him whoop me for sure. The old bastard likes it too much."

"Mike, Shut up and turn to chapter twelve."

# Chapter 4

## *Cultivate Your Garden*

*A summer garden is a glorious thing but gardens aren't just ever perpetuating flower machines. They will flower endlessly and give the caretaker and passer-byers, alike, continuous delight but they need to be groomed and cultivated. Care needs to be taken. The joy of work has to be added not just sun, water and time.*

**The Reilly front yard is in full bloom.** Heavy pink peonies droop with bowed heads, nodding politely to everyone that entered through the gate. Ma Reilly took special care of her garden. To some it seemed like it was some sort of an incongruity considering her other, shall we say, less lady-like pursuits of running a brothal. Every spring she had the front porch and white picket fence scraped and painted. She wanted them to be the perfect back drop and frame for her welcoming house. Grams was proud of her garden.

The gate slammed behind Katharine. She strolled casually into the front yard. Without breaking stride she picked a giant peony head as she walked towards the house. She put it to her nose, smelled deeply and tossed it into the bushes a few steps later. She could have cherished and saved the gorgeous blossom; she could have closed the gate gently behind herself with grace; she could have tip toed into the house and spread out her books and at least pretended to be deep in thought pondering over homework but not Katharine. Katharine had a defiant streak especially when it came to dealing with her mother. Ma Reilly often saw the belligerence and selfishness that was lurking just beneath the surface. She thought of her daughter as contentious but the fact is that most, called her a darling with a sweet disposition, especially when the anticipation of something she wanted peeked her interest. When the mood suited her she was cooperative, kind and even generous. Most of the town folk had known her this way but her mother never knew which Katharine she would get from moment to moment.

From a distance Ma Reilly snarled loudly, "Katharine, where have you been?. . . Katharine. Your teacher called and said you ain't been to school all day. Beth said you gave her a note to take to your teacher sayin' I kept you home 'cause you were sick. Katharine . . . where are you?"

Katharine was in one of her – if I ignore her she will leave me alone – moods. She flicked on the TV and surfed for something that might entertain her for the moment. Homework would wait, if at all.

* * *

Katharine had an interesting face. Her eye brows were plucked into pencil-thin lines which gave her a rigid look of constant worry. Her hair was blond though the dark roots revealed her ill kept secret; her eyes were green, as green as spring grass. Her generous smile shone through any worry she might have. It was this smile that made hard and fast friends on impact. Most of the town saw the smile but the family saw the worry.

"Katharine Reilly, I know I am only your auntie, but you are just like your mother. You worry and then you give up on everything. She would worry about tests and exams and then she'd skip school and go hang out with friends at the bar or pool hall. She never even finished grade nine because she gave it no mind.

"I figure you had better pull up your socks otherwise you are going to marry some guy that is no good for you and ruin your life. Do you know that your mother had an abortion from Doc Miller years before you were born? It's a good job she married your dad when you came along otherwise who knows what would have happened to her. It's such a shame your daddy died so young."

Katharine's eyes glazed over while her aunt Dorothy rambled on and on about what her mom should have done and how she is following down the same path to ruin. Katharine heard it all before from different family members, from the priest, from the guidance councillor at school. She just didn't seem to care much about how her life would turn out. Katharine's mind began to wander while Aunt Dorothy persisted with her monologue. She was lying on a beach in the south of France with a fancy cocktail. The surf rolled gently in the distance past the brilliant blue pool. It was cool in the sun where she was. There were plenty of people around to take care of her and feed the fantasy of being loved.

"Katharine, have you heard a single word I have said? You are following down the same path as your mother."

* * *

"Mrs. Reilly, you had better come down to the station right away to collect your daughter. The problem? The problem is Ma'am that your daughter has been caught stealing again."

Chapter 5

# Mike's Got No Pa

*It was another dog day afternoon in July. It was a still morning and the day had already grown sultry; hotter than any summer day should be. Not even the mosquitoes dared to leave the confines of the cool shade. Heat like this leaves lots of time to wonder about your place in the community and family. Heat slows you down to look at your roots.*

**Chris and Mike wandered down the hill** past the grey old barn to the creek. Investigating the slithering approach of a muskrat could not pull the boys from the creek's embrace. They laid half submerged, lollygagging the time away till hunger would send them home. The day was only worth hanging in the shade. Every free minute of every free day was spent building dams and fishing, out of ear shot of anyone. There would be plenty of crayfish and snakes and if they were lucky they would find a salamander or a dead seagull.

"I ain't sure I like summer much better than the school year, "Mike said off the cuff. "I figure one is a trade off for the other. Summer's too hot and winter's too cold, summer ya always got extra chores to do and winter ya got school and home work. Summer we could go on a holiday but we never go nowhere and I don't want to go nowhere with Grams and old man Barker anyhow. Winter there ain't no holidays except for Christmas and I hate Christmas and I don't much care for the rest of the holiday either 'cause ya gotta have a place to go to have a holiday. No point in havin' a holiday stayin' home in the snow.

"I don't much care that old man Finlan passed us both. I know you worked hard Chris and you helped me plenty but I still figure he just passed me so as he won't have to have me in his class again next year. What am I going to use algebra for anyway? Grams says I'm going to be dead before I'm thirty, just like my Pa. I figure there's not much use for algebra in hell anyway."

"Mike, how come you got no Dad? I know your Grams said your Mom died in a car accident but how come you got no Dad?"

"I don't know, I ain't ever knowed my Pa. Grams said she scared him off 'cause he was no good and only worth hangin'. Old man Barker said he's in jail for murder and he ain't ever gettin' out – killed a cop while robbin' a bank or something like that.

"I seen a dead dog one time. It was like a big slab a meat with fur still on it; it just laid there kinda cold and didn't move none. I couldn't imagine shootin' no cop dead. I could never forgive myself; I'd kill myself first.

"One time when I was just little I killed a porcupine. He was chewin' on the house one night and Grams made me go out with a broom and shoo it away. I pushed him and he wouldn't run away so I wacked him. That sure made him wake up and think but he only sauntered away as if he was going to church on a hot Sunday morning so I give him a hefty wack to get him movin' faster. All I was trying to do was tell him to git and never come back but I guess I wacked him too hard and I killed 'im. First I thought that maybe I just knocked him out but in the morning I found him dead. He weren't ever comin' back to chew on our house that was for sure. I buried him out beside a tree and will never forget his little pink tongue stickin' out lickin' for a last breath and his little black eyes lookin' up at me asking. "Why did you kill me you mean old boy. I was only a little critter lookin' for my dinner.' I cried, without anyone seein' me, for days. I don't know if I ever forgave myself.

"I seen my Ma when she was dead. Grams told me to get out of the house but I peeked in her bedroom when Doc. Miller was goin' in. She was all white and still. She didn't have a smile and she didn't have a frown. She just looked like she was asleep but I knew she wasn't ever going to come back to us. I was out hangin' with friends that afternoon. I was just havin' fun. Maybe if I had just come home, even just a bit earlier. Maybe if I had. . ."

Chris quickly interrupted. "I never saw a dead person before, only in the movies. I killed a toad once with a firecracker, blew him to smithereens. I didn't cry. I just thought it was funny. Now that I'm older I couldn't kill a toad that way. I never seen a dead person though. My grandpa died but I was just little. I hardly even remember him dying; I've never seen a dead person."

"I don't know if my Dad is dead or alive. I saw a picture of him one time and I know he wouldn'ta killed no cop. He looked like a nice sort a guy leaning on his brand new Impala. I'm saving up for a car but I ain't gunna rob no banks. I figure old man Barker just made that up to bug me. My Pa wouldn'ta killed no cop. My Ma never told me anything much about him but I just know he would'ta killed no cop, at least not on purpose. Maybe he robbed a bank or done something stupid, who hasn't."

"The problem is Mike that one stupid thing leads to another stupid thing and to another and another. My Dad says the trick is to not do the first stupid thing in the first place. He says you gotta keep doing smart things and there won't be any time to do the stupid thing that leads to the next stupid thing. Something like that anyway. That's what he was telling me when we got caught skippin' school. That was one of those dumb things.' he said."

"Skippin' school might be dumb Chris, but it's only a little dumb. Everyone skips school at some point. I bet half the teachers skipped school when they were young and they turned out to be teachers an' they never robbed no bank or killed no body."

Time dwindled on, evening invaded the distant hills; the heat disappeared and cool finally set in as the day deepened to dark. The boys finally found the motivation that sent them home.

Chapter 6

# Naked as a Jay Bird

*It is the effortless unfettered pleasures that bring out the joys in life and make existence worth living.  Without relishing the simplicity of a gentle breeze fluttering a leaf, a wave gurgling under a rock stroon shore line, without beaming at the innocence of a butterfly shedding its winter cocoon there is no point in simply filling in time.*

**"Don't you just love corn season?** I love strawberries; I love the sweet tiny peas when they first come out and I love fresh tomatoes sun hot off the vine but oh my gosh I love corn season the most. Some like their corn with butter, salt and pepper but I like my corn naked."

Ma Reilly laughed out loud and slapped her thigh. "Katharine, I can just picture you eatin' your corn naked. Since you was just a little girl you always liked bein' naked. I would put you out on the clothes line in your harness so you could play and have the run of the backyard and I didn't have to watch you every minute. I would come out a few minutes later and find you naked as a jay bird. The only thing that you would have on is your harness. You always had to be naked no matter who was around. I would put you in your swim suit and put you in your little pool and you would get naked. I would put you to bed in your PJs and I would find you naked in the morning. I bet you still sleep in your nudidity. I couldn't keep your clothes on you. There was nothin' bashful about you girl. You was as sweet and innocent as a little bug back then. I don't know what happened. One day you was a sweet child and the next you was pregnant."

"Ma, you just can't let it lie can you. You always gotta bring it up. One minute you are saying what a delight I was; pretty and innocent and then you gotta bring it up again and again. I didn't get pregnant because I was naked. I got pregnant because..."

"Katharine, I know the facts of life but it starts with takin' your clothes off. You took your clothes off for half the boys on the street. Don't think that I didn't know what you was up to takin' those boys out behind the shed and them payin' you just to look at your privates. I knew what you was doin'. You were like a cat in heat even back then. You made it just a bit too easy for them. Sellin' yourself one peek at a time for twenty five cents. I know you don't get pregnant just by gettin' naked but you can't get pregnant if you leave all your clothes on. It's your fault that you got pregnant. You should'a left your nickers up."

"Ma, you know how I got pregnant and it wasn't from one of the boys taking a peek at my privates. You know how it was. I want you to say it, Ma. I learned my tricks for earning extra money from you Ma. Say the fat old bastard's name Ma. If Pa had still been with us he would have killed him; maybe even you too. Fat old bastard even farted when he did it to me and what did you do; nothing and it didn't just happen once Ma.

"He was the one that taught me to show my privates Ma. He gave me twenty-five cents the first time, Ma. I kind of liked having the twenty-five cents. You never gave me no spending money. Then as time went on he touched me and then one time when he thought you were out he raped me and you didn't do anything. I know you were home but all you did was pretend you never heard nothing. What did you think he was doing in my bedroom, Ma?

"How can I forgive you for that Ma. You were too busy worrying about all of those people that you called your friends that constantly filled the house. You might as well have been running a whore house the way you had so many of 'his' friends over. All the late drinking and loud music. How much did he pay you Ma for havin' his way with me? If you don't say his name out loud Ma I'm gunna kill myself. I swear Ma I'm gunna kill myself."

Chapter 7

# The Blur of Time

*Contrary to common understanding, time is not a constant. How many minutes in the day do you lose while daydreaming that never really existed? Just how many milliseconds are there in a lifetime and how many of them evaporate between moments of fear and anger? Days, months even years whiz by like there was no yesterday, today or even tomorrow. Days are marked off the calendar whether a moment is remembered or not. Months are ripped from the nail of time and discarded as uncelebrated events and missed opportunities. Years sometimes slip by in a joyless blink. What is the point of experiencing this phenomenon called time if it is not the joyous activity of divine Life's living.*

**Mike jumped up from his easy chair** and reached for the phone before the second ring. "Hey Chris, man it's great to hear your voice. How long has it been? Almost two years. So you're back at school working on your masters in English Literature?  I love all the letters you send me about the books you are reading.  I have actually read a few of them. I was reading one by Atwood the other night. It's kind of interesting. I might just finish this one.

"You will never guess what happened to me the other night.  You can use it in one of your stories. I was driving down the highway heading south back into town with an empty truck. It had been a long haul and I was tired, maybe even fed up with the cold, the traffic and a numb bum let alone a numb mind. I have long since given up hoping that I would be given the truck with the good heater in it. Two years of driving doesn't give me seniority enough to be given any perks. At least I have a radio, to keep me company.  I had to jam a wire clothes hanger into the antenna where it was broken off to get any tunes but it works ok.

"Anyway I was driving along and I slammed on the brakes and backed up to what looked like an old man stooped over his rear tire.  "You got a flat buddy, you need some help? Let me take a look at it for you. I just got my working clothes on. You don't want to get your good pants dirty kneeling in the gravel.

"It was kind of a spooky thing, this shadowy figure stood up and looked me straight in the eye. I could have just about fallen over with shock. There he was as plain as day. Old man Barker looked at me and said, 'Sure would be obliged if you helped me change this thing. I'd be happy to give you a few bucks for your trouble.'

"He looked up at me like he was looking at a stranger and didn't flinch. The fact is I hardly recognized him myself. Had he lost some weight or was it that he was clean shaven and wore a pressed suit? He just seemed like a kind, helpless old guy that needed a hand. He seemed softer and more, well, more something, more kind. There didn't seem to be any sign of the brute that I thought I knew. Barker must have seen my mouth drop open when he turned and saw me in the bright light of the street lamp. I took a few too many beatings from that old bastard and here I am pulled over helping him like he was some old friend.

"You remember the time I was late feeding the pigs and Grams told him to give me a beating? Well he did and a bad one too. Well I almost hit him in the back of the head with a shovel after he turned and walked away leaving me lying in a sobbing heap with a bleeding lip. It was one of those – I don't want to go to hell for killing a man – moments that flashes through your mind. It is one of those milliseconds that last for the longest time. I remember I tossed the shovel to the ground and walked away with mostly only bruised pride and bruised ribs. I was bigger and stronger then. Not like the first times he gave me a lickin'.

"That last time I could have been his match but even as he took his hand to me I knew I would soon be leaving Grams and I would be shut of them both. Not slugging him with the shovel was the smartest thing that I never did. In a flash I remembered what you said your Dad told you. 'One stupid thing leads to another stupid thing.' or something like that. That was years ago but there was a more important issue mullin' over in my head. It's kind of funny and whether it's valid or not I had my Dad's reputation to live down. I kept saying that he couldn't have killed a cop. Remember I told you that old man Barker told me that my dad killed a cop. Maybe he did or maybe he didn't but I couldn't let him down nonetheless. I never knew my Pa but I still would want him to be proud of me. I guess smacking Barker in the back of the head with a shovel would be a stupid thing to do and then people would only say I was just like my dad.

"Sorry I'm jabbering on so much. It has been three years or maybe even more since I last saw Barker. My Grams finally got fed up with him and kicked him out; I think he must have raised a hand to her one time too many. I think he actually left town. I didn't really much care and never thought about him much after that. Anytime his name ever came up at Grams I just referred to him as the fat old bastard. Grams gave me a bunch of his stuff that he left behind including a pair of nice black shoes. Oh man wouldn't it have been funny if I had his old shoes on that night? It is kind of funny that I fit his shoes now don't you think? I always thought that he was much bigger than I was. It is one of them tricks of the imagination – the house you grew up in seems awfully small now or the roller coaster that scared the bajeebers out of you was actually not all that tall or fast. Man you remember how terrified I was of that man and next thing you know I'm standing there beside him and he looks like a regular old man that couldn't be much nicer.

"Just about everything else that was his I gave away or chucked out. I had no need for his fancy going-to-meeting clothes and I didn't read much back then so I gave away most of his books. Remember they were just cheap Zane Grey paper backs but there were quite a few of them. You remember that we took some down to the creek. One page after another we ripped them apart and laid the pages gently on the water and watched them disappear. There was no ceremony or anger or anything like that. We just watched the pages lie on the water like dead leaves and go for a gentle ride. I remember you laughing and telling me that some old beaver would gather them up and paste them on the walls of his den and his little baby beavers would all grow up reading cheap cowboy novels. Did you know that Zane Grey's real name was Pearl, Pearl Zane Grey. I had an aunt named Pearl once.

"It is amazing how many thoughts and fragments of time you can pack into the few minutes it takes to change a tire. My mind flashed to my Mom and how much I still missed her and how things might have been different if she was still alive and how come she hated Barker so much. I thought of some of those other stupid things that lead to other stupid things like stealing at the corner store and how I had to then lie to my Mom why I didn't go to that corner store to pick up the milk for her and pretend that I just wanted to go for a long walk to the other store and how I used to duck around the corner when I saw old lady Keeler from the store, walking my way. She said she wouldn't call the police if I stopped stealing and if I started doing nice things for folk like helping them out from time to time. I figured, even back then, that she gave me a big break and I thanked her under my breath. I figure I should go back and tell her in person one day.

"Yah, yah, what happened to Barker? I'm getting to that; I told him, "Well Mister, she's all put back together and you're ready to roll. Let me put this in your trunk for you. No. No, I don't need any money for doing a good turn. Pass it on to someone else one day. Old man Barker turned back towards me, looked me straight in the eye, hesitated, paused and seemed to search for the right words. . . . 'Are you sure I can't give you something? It was very kind of you young man. The world sure could use a few more like you.' He reached out and put five bucks in my coat pocket. He patted me on the shoulder and said, 'Thanks again.'

I was dumbfounded and before I could say anything more he slowly pulled back onto the highway and drove away. I stood there with my hands in my pockets and watched his tail lights disappear; he was out of my life once again. I stood there mumbling out loud to myself kickin' gravel. "What a fool I am. I coulda' said something to him. I coulda' told him that I recognized him or that I finally forgive him. I coulda' said how's things or I coulda' said I got your shoes and you can't have 'm back. Coulda', coulda', coulda' is all that dragged through my tired brain. At least I didn't say "Fix your own damn tire you fat old bastard!" Thank God I didn't say that.

Chapter 8

# *Slug in the Sun*

*Last night there was a very gentle, sparse rain; even though meagre it was glorious. It was hardly enough to quench the early September thirst that was mounting in the dry meadow. The swale behind the barn is dry though resilient and the last to stay green. Some roots are deep and even though life looks exhausted and ready to expire it is most often only dormant. The aroma of fresh grass once again fills the air and life is new again; some more fragile than others are sadly brittle and dead. Some plants spring back to life with no hesitation and others are tentative vacillating in their commitment to what might be a temporary reprieve. The inevitability of new is born.*

**"I brought you some flowers, Ma.** They are just wild ones but I picked them myself. It's amazing how they are in full bloom and all the grass around looks dead. They must have real good roots. I wonder why they all can't have good roots? I got the legs of my pants wet walkin' out into the field to pick'm. It rained earlier today but only enough to get the tall grass wet and then the sun burst out again.

"After the sun had been out for a little while I plucked a half dried up slug off of the sidewalk and tossed it in the bushes. I don't know if it was dead or not. It must have slugged its way out from under the bushes while it was raining. Before it could get across the sidewalk the sun came out and dried him out. You could tell where he came from on account of his long silver trail that he left behind him; it shone in the sunlight. He must have come to a slow grinding halt and stopped right there. The poor little guy must have said to himself, 'I don't know why I done such a stupid thing. I can't make another slither and here I am stuck in the middle of this dry hot sidewalk and I'm gunna die. I just can't go no further and then along came this giant guy and tossed me back into the moist shade of the bush.' It's funny that I mighta saved the little guy's life.

"Sorry it's been so long since I visited you last. I've

been driving truck lots, mostly the run up north. It takes one day up and one back and then I do some shorter runs here and there and then I turn around and do it all over again a few days later. Seems to me I've been doing that for a bit too long. I will do it till something else comes along, till something else feels right. Ma, it's kind of like learning how to trust that the rain will come and the flowers won't die. I never thought of it but the grass always comes back. No matter how dry it gets.

"I make sure I'm back on Tuesday and Thursday nights for my classes. I'm gettin' my grade twelve math so as I can take the locksmith course that I always wanted to take. The other one that I'm taking is grade twelve English. I don't have to take that one but Chris kinda' pushed me to take it. He tells me about some of the things he is reading in college and they sound pretty interesting. Who woulda' thought I would be reading Steinbeck's 'The Winter of Our Discontent' without a teacher making me. It's all about loss of integrity and morality, at least that's what the cover flaps say. I've only started it but I already know I'll finish it because it's so interesting.

"Ma, I sometimes still wonder why you left us. Grams still tells people you died in a car accident but I figured out a long time ago that you killed yourself. I just didn't want to tell you that I knew. Things must have been real bad for you for a long time to do that, Ma. I thought about it myself a few times but I figured out that the rain always comes; I'm ok now. I am sorry if I was part of that bad time and caused you any trouble, Ma. I wish I could talk to

Grams about it but she just mostly shuts me out and never wants to talk about you. She's got a picture of you on her dresser but she never wants to talk about you.

"I visit Grams from time to time. She's getting old and sometimes forgets more than she remembers. I think it is her way of coping with you being gone even after all this time. She pretty much lives alone now. She's only got her pup living with her. She called it Weasel. She says the damn dog is the only one stupid enough to stick with her. I figure she likes her pup better than she ever liked me. I stack fire wood and cut her grass every time I go by and I take her some Kentucky Fried Chicken almost every time. She still loves it just like when you were with us. I remember you and her would toss bones onto each other's plates and count them up to see who had the most so as you knew who would get the last piece. Do you remember the time when your Weasel sneaked up and stole the last piece because you were laughing so hard about who would get it?

"Well there's not much more to say, Ma. Everything is pretty much the same as it was the last time I visited. My rabbit's havin' babies. I got a little white one with black blotches and made a cage. My landlady is real nice. She doesn't mind me havin' rabbits. 'Just as long as they don't bark.' she said she don't mind. She's a nice lady. She kinda reminds me of you. She's pretty and has lots of energy, like you when I was just little. You would like her I'm sure. Her husband died sometime back so I help her out around the place.

"Well there's not much else to say. I guess I had better go now. I got to drive north in the morning and I got a few things to do before I go.

"Oh I forgot to tell you that I ran into old man Barker. I told you that Grams had kicked him out sometime ago. Well I stopped to help an old guy who had a flat tire on the highway and it turned out to be him. He's just a harmless old guy now. I know you didn't like him much but somehow he turned ok. He just looked like any nice old man you would see. He didn't recognize me none and I didn't want to get into anything with him so I just let him drive off.

"I figure it would have cost me too much to drag up the past. I was trying to forgive him for the longest time. Now that I seen him as an old man, fragile and even kind of innocent I just can't hold a grudge anymore. Ma, it turns out he has good roots after all. I just want to move on and not think about him and how nasty he was. It's kind of like tossing a slug into the bushes to see if he will live or not. It doesn't take any energy to toss him and it doesn't take any energy to just let him go on his way and forgive him.

"Anyway Ma, I gotta go now. I'll come back and visit again sometime soon. I love you, Ma."

*The End*

**Richard M. Grove,** otherwise known to friends by his nickname, Tai, was born in Hamilton, Ontario, Canada in 1953. He is now a Brighton artist, writer, photographer and publisher, father of two daughters and married to

*Photo taken by photographer, brother Christopher.*

writer/editor Kim. Richard edits and publishes all genre from his company Hidden Brook Press at <u>www.hidden-brookpress.com</u>. He is the President of the Canada Cuba Literary Alliance as well as the Founding President of the Brighton Arts Council.

He has had over 100 poems published in many different periodicals around the world as well as having been published in over 30 anthologies – the most recent Beyond the Seventh Morning featured 3 poems and 15 photographs. He is the artist and author of over 15 books.

He was an active member of the Canadian Poetry Association for almost ten years serving on the executive for seven years including five as President. Richard is also the founder of the Canadian Poet Registry, an archival information website that lists Canadian poets including biographical information, their book titles and awards. One can view this website at http://www.hidden-brookpress.com/Registry.htm. Richard has given speeches, readings and workshops on poetry and publishing at literary festivals in Canada, Cuba, Germany and New Zealand.

Since graduating from Ontario College of Art, in 1984, Richard has exhibited in more than twenty, solo and group exhibitions in Hamilton, Toronto, Boston, Calgary and Grand Prairie. He has his paintings in over thirty corporate collections across Canada.

# Books by Richard M. Grove

*Some of the latter books
are now available on Amazon
and other e-stores.*

Beyond Fear and Anger
Poems For Jack
A View of Contrasts: Cuba Poems
The Mind Body Connection
Sky Over Presqu'ile
terra firma
Oxido Rojo
Substantiality
Cuba Trip e-book
A Spiritual Study of Body
The Family Reunion
From Cross Hill
Psycho Babble and the Consternations of Life
a trip to banes, cuba, 2002
Trapped in Paradise – Views of My Cuba
North of Belleville (*with James Deahl*)
In This We Hear the Light (*with John B. Lee*)
The Importance of Good Roots

www.ingramcontent.com/pod-product-compliance
Lightning Source LLC
Chambersburg PA
CBHW061459210726
48287CB00007B/2573